THE SHAKESPEARE STORIES

ANDREW MATTHEWS
& TONY ROSS

4 BOOKS IN ONE!

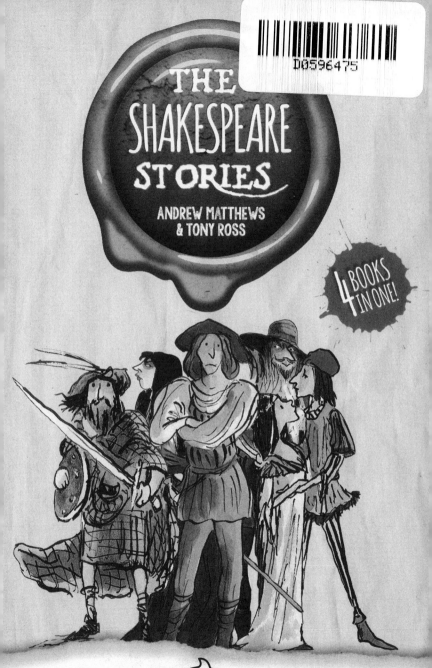

Silver Dolphin
San Diego, California

Silver Dolphin Books
An imprint of Printers Row Publishing Group
10350 Barnes Canyon Road, Suite 100, San Diego, CA 92121
www.silverdolphinbooks.com

This text was first published in Great Britain in 2001 by The Watts Publishing Group

Text © Andrew Matthews, 2001
Illustrations © Tony Ross, 2002

Printers Row Publishing Group is a division of Readerlink Distribution Services, LLC.
Silver Dolphin Books is a registered trademark of Readerlink Distribution Services, LLC.

All notations of errors or omissions should be addressed to Silver Dolphin Books, Editorial Department
at the above address. All other correspondence (author inquiries, permissions) concerning
the content of this book should be addressed to Orchard Books, Carmelite House,
50 Victoria Embankment, London EC4Y 0DZ, UK.

ISBN: 978-1-68412-162-5

Manufactured, printed, and assembled in Crawfordsville, IN, USA. LSC/03/17.

21 20 19 18 17 1 2 3 4 5

contents

Who was William Shakespeare?   4

The Globe Theatre   6

Much Ado About Nothing   9

The Taming of the Shrew   71

Macbeth   133

Romeo and Juliet   195

Who Was William Shakespeare?

William Shakespeare was an English poet and playwright whose treasured works have been performed throughout the world and translated into most languages. Although much is known about his writings, Shakespeare himself remains a bit of a mystery.

Records suggest he was baptized on April 26, 1564, so his birthdate would have been a few days prior. Shakespeare grew up 100 miles northwest of London in a town called Stratford-upon-Avon. His father, John, was a leatherworker, and his mother, Mary Arden, was from a prominent local family. Shakespeare attended the local grammar school that would have included Latin and Greek curriculum, which would have exposed him to classic plays. In November 1582, at the age of 18, Shakespeare married Anne Hathaway, the daughter of a local farmer. They had three children, Susanna and twins Hamnet and Judith.

Shakespeare's life revolved around two locations: Stratford-upon-Avon and London. In London, he had a successful career as an actor, writer, and part owner of the company Lord Chamberlain's Men. In 1599, Shakespeare and Lord Chamberlain's Men built the Globe Theatre where they performed plays. In the years 1590-1613, Shakespeare wrote his most well-known works. Early plays were comedies and histories, and he wrote mostly tragedies until 1608 including *Hamlet*, *King Lear*, and *Macbeth*.

On April 23, 1616, William Shakespeare died in Stratford-upon-Avon. Over 400 years later, his works are celebrated around the world through festivals, read by students, and analyzed and reinterpreted by scholars. Shakespeare's plays are the most performed in the world, and their commentary on human emotion and conflict has transcended time.

The Globe Theatre

Some of Shakespeare's most famous plays were first performed at the Globe Theatre, which was built on the South Bank of the River Thames in 1599.

Going to the Globe was a different experience from going to the theater today. The building was roughly circular in shape, but with flat sides. Because the Globe was an open-air theater, plays were put on only during daylight hours in spring and summer. People paid one English penny to stand in the central space and watch a play, and this part of the audience became known as the groundlings because they stood on the ground. A place in the tiers of seating beneath the thatched roof, where there was a slightly better view and less chance of being rained on, cost extra.

The Elizabethans did not bathe very often, and the audiences at the Globe were smelly. Fine ladies and gentlemen in the more expensive seats sniffed perfume and bags of sweetly scented herbs to cover the stink rising from the groundlings.

There were no actresses on the stage; all the female characters in Shakespeare's plays were performed by boys wearing wigs and makeup. Audiences were not well-behaved. People clapped and cheered when their favorite actors came on stage; bad actors were jeered at and sometimes pelted with whatever came to hand. Most Londoners worked hard to make a living and in their precious free time they liked to be entertained. Shakespeare understood the magic of the theater so well that today, almost four hundred years after his death, his plays still cast a spell over the thousands of people that go to see them.

❋ ❋ ❋

Much Ado About Nothing

A shakespeare story

For Patrick, Penny and Leila, with love
A. M.

RETOLD BY ANDREW MATTHEWS

ILLUSTRATED BY TONY ROSS

Cast List

Don Pedro

Prince of Aragon

Claudio

Companion of Don Pedro

Benedick

Companion of Don Pedro

Leonato

Governor of Messina

Hero

Leonato's daughter

Beatrice

Leonato's niece

The Scene

Sicily in the sixteenth century

Sigh no more, ladies, sigh no more,
Men were deceivers ever,
One foot in sea, and one on shore,
To one thing constant never.

Balthazar; II.iii.

much Ado About Nothing

In the house of Leonato, Governor of Messina, all was fuss and flutter. The governor's old friend Don Pedro, Prince of Aragon, and several of his captains had stayed at the house some months earlier, on their way to war. With the war safely won, the prince had decided to visit again on his return.

Shortly before Don Pedro's arrival, two lovely young women hurried down to the main courtyard of the governor's house. One was Hero, Leonato's only child; the other was her cousin Beatrice. Though the two were closer than sisters, they had little in common. Dark-haired Hero's innocent blue eyes matched her mild-mannered sweetness. Beatrice had fair hair, a sharp mind, and an even sharper tongue.

"Lord Claudio fought well, by all accounts," Beatrice remarked to her cousin as they descended a staircase. "You took quite a fancy to him last time he was here, didn't you?"

"Just as you took a fancy to Lord Benedick!" said Hero, blushing.

Beatrice rolled her eyes. "Benedick is the most irritating man I've ever met!"

"Why?" said Hero. "Because he's as witty as you?"

"Because he *thinks* he's as witty as me!" Beatrice growled. "If he lived off his wit, he would die of starvation."

Hero and Beatrice reached the courtyard

and stood beside Leonato, just as the prince's party rode in through the gates and dismounted. Don Pedro was flanked by Claudio, whose brown curls glowed in the sunlight, and Benedick, whose mouth wore its customary cynical smile.

Behind them came
Don John, the prince's
half-brother, with his
servant, Borachio.

After embracing
Leonato, Don Pedro
stared in wonder
at Hero.

"You've grown so tall
while I've been away!"
he exclaimed.

Hero, who was gazing at Claudio, who
was gazing back at her, made no reply.

"Or have we grown shorter, my lord?" quipped Benedick. "Perhaps the heavy armor we've been wearing has squashed us."

"Why are you prattling on, Benedick? No one's listening," Beatrice said sharply.

Benedick mocked her with a bow. "Ah, Lady Beatrice, as scornful as ever!"

"That's hardly surprising," Beatrice said. "When I'm with you, I see so much to be scornful of."

She turned away to follow Don Pedro and her uncle into the house.

Benedick nudged Claudio in the ribs.

"Pity the man who marries her, eh, Claudio?" he chuckled. "*Claudio?*"

Claudio was glassy-eyed.

"Did you see Hero?" he murmured.

"Yes! Pretty girl, not as pretty as her cousin, but—"

"Hero is the most wonderful person in the world!" Claudio sighed. Benedick peered closely at his friend. "You haven't fallen in love, have you?"

"Head over heels!" Claudio groaned.

"Ha!" scoffed Benedick. "You'll be telling me you want to marry Hero next."

"If I don't, I'll never be happy again," Claudio said gloomily.

Don Pedro appeared at the door.

"What's keeping you both?" he inquired.

"Claudio is in love with Hero and wants to marry her!" declared Benedick.

"My lord, the day you hear that I wish to marry, set me up as a target and shoot me with arrows."

"Is this true, Claudio?" the prince said.

"Yes," said Claudio. "I didn't notice Hero before, because I could think only of the war, but now that I've seen her beauty, I can't live without her! What shall I do, my lord?"

Don Pedro placed a hand on Claudio's shoulder.

"Leave this to me," he said. "Leonato is holding a masked ball tonight. I'll dance with Hero and explain your feelings for her. If she feels the same, I'll ask Leonato for her hand on your behalf."

Claudio beamed.

Benedick muttered under his breath.

✳ ✳ ✳

That night, the ballroom of the governor's house swirled with music and dancers. Claudio stood on tiptoe and peered anxiously at Don Pedro and Hero as they swept across the dance floor.

On the opposite side of the room, Benedick, in a hare mask, was in conversation with Beatrice, whose mask resembled an owl's face.

Benedick had adopted a strange accent to conceal his identity. Beatrice knew perfectly well who he was, but pretended that she did not.

"Won't you tell me your name, stranger?" she pleaded.

"Pardon me, but no," said Benedick.

"You're as provoking as Lord Benedick!" grumbled Beatrice.

"Lord Benedick?" Benedick said. "Who is he?"

"He's the prince's jester and the dullest of fools," said Beatrice. "People laugh more behind his back than they do at his jokes."

"If I meet him, I'll tell him you said so,"
Benedick said.

"Please do!" said Beatrice, slipping
away between the dancing couples.

Benedick was stung.

"So that's her opinion of me!" he
thought. "A jester and a dull fool."

He frowned, puzzled.

"But why should I care what Beatrice thinks of me?" he asked himself. "We can't stand each other—can we?"

Meanwhile, Don Pedro presented Hero to Claudio, while Leonato looked on in smiling approval.

"The lady is wooed and won," said the prince. "You'll be married in the family chapel the day after tomorrow," Leonato declared. These words were caught by a man wearing a fox's head mask.

"My master ought to know of this,"
thought the man, threading through
the throng.

He was Don John's servant, Borachio.
As Don Pedro raised a goblet of wine to
toast Hero and Claudio,
Benedick chanced
by. He had
removed his
mask to reveal
a glum face.

"Celebrate with us, Benedick!" Don Pedro urged.

"Forgive me, my lord, but I'm not in the mood," said Benedick. "I'm escaping from Lady Beatrice. I've had enough of her for one night."

Don Pedro smiled at Benedick's departing back. "What a couple Benedick and Beatrice would make," he said. Leonato guffawed. "They would talk themselves mad in a week!" "I suspect that they're fonder of each other than they realize," said Don Pedro.

"If we convinced Benedick that Beatrice was in love with him, and Beatrice that Benedick loved her, nature would do the rest."

"But how could we convince them, my lord?" Claudio said.

Don Pedro lowered his voice, and the others huddled round like conspirators.

* * *

Borachio discovered Don John skulking in his room.

"You should have come to the ball, my lord," Borachio said.

Don John scowled. "Watching the prince being flattered would have sickened me! Because our father married his mother and not mine, he rules while I serve. I daren't challenge him, but if I could find a way to hurt him and his fawning friends . . ."

"I may know a way, my lord," Borachio smirked. "I've learned that Lady Hero is to marry Lord Claudio. I've also learned that Lady Hero's chambermaid, Margaret, is sweet on me, and that's given me an idea."

"What idea?" asked Don John.

Borachio answered at length, and what he said brought a cruel smile to his master's lips.

* * *

The next morning, Benedick strolled through the governor's gardens deep in thought.

"Why does love turn people into fools?" he mused. "A few days ago, Claudio was a courageous soldier, now he's a drooling lapdog. It will take a special kind of woman to win my love—beautiful, wise, witty, well-to-do. Where will I find someone like that?"

Benedick followed a path between two hedges, and from the opposite side of the hedge to his left, he heard Don Pedro chatting with Leonato and Claudio.

The subject
of their
conversation
stopped Benedick
in his tracks,
but the hedge
prevented him
from seeing the
twinkle in the
men's eyes as
they spoke.

"So your
niece Beatrice
loves Benedick,
Leonato?" said
Don Pedro.

"To distraction,
my lord,"
Leonato replied.

"It's pitiful to hear her at night, whispering his name and weeping."

"But she behaves as if she detests Benedick!" said Claudio.

"Pretense!" Leonato assured him. "She knows that if Benedick finds out that she loves him, he'll mock her for it. To avoid the humiliation, she keeps her breaking heart hidden."

"Should I talk to Benedick and tell him to be gentle with her?" inquired Don Pedro.

"I don't know what to do for the best, my lord," Leonato confided. "I'm afraid that Beatrice's passion for Benedick will drive her out of her wits."

The three men sighed heavily.

"Let's go inside," said Don Pedro. "A good idea might come to us over dinner."

For several minutes Benedick paced
up and down, chin in hand, while his
mind churned.

"Beatrice loves me!" he thought. "Poor
girl, I can't stand by and watch her suffer.
She must be rescued, and the only rescue
is . . . for me to woo her!"

"Benedick?" said a voice.

Benedick looked
round and saw
Beatrice behind
him. He
searched her
face for signs
of secret love.

"The prince
sent me to ask
you in to dinner,"
Beatrice said.

"It wasn't my idea. I don't care whether you have dinner or go without."

"Thank you for taking the trouble to find me," said Benedick.

"If it had been any trouble, I wouldn't have bothered!" Beatrice snapped.

She turned on her heel and flounced off.

"If it had been any trouble, I wouldn't have bothered," Benedick repeated softly. "There's a hidden meaning in those words . . . somewhere. She loves me, sure as can be!"

It did not occur to him to wonder why he felt so delighted.

✳ ✳ ✳

On her way back to the house, Beatrice
noticed Hero and her maid, Ursula, seated
on the edge of a fountain that was ringed
by statues on pedestals. Beatrice went to

join them but ducked
behind the nearest
statue when Ursula
shrieked, "Lord
Benedick? In love
with Lady Beatrice?"

"Don Pedro told me
so," said Hero. "He asked me
to mention it to Beatrice, but I refused.
She'll never return Benedick's love."

"Why ever not?" Ursula exclaimed.
"He's a handsome enough fellow."

"Beatrice is too cold and proud to

surrender herself to any man," said Hero.
"If she knew about Benedick, she would
make a laughingstock of him no matter
how sick with love he is."

"True!" Ursula agreed. "Better for the
poor man to die from love than from the
lashing of Lady Beatrice's tongue."

Beatrice's eyes bulged.

"Cold, proud—*me*?" she thought. "I'll show them how wrong they are. I'll save Benedick's life—by loving him. Don't die yet, dearest Benedick!"

She had never thought of Benedick as *dearest* before.

✳ ✳ ✳

Late that night, Don Pedro answered a knock on his door and found himself facing his half-brother. "What is it?" asked Don Pedro. "Wake your friend Claudio," Don John said. "I have something to show him." "At this hour?" Don John nodded. "If I told him, he wouldn't believe me, and nor would you," he said grimly. "You must see for yourselves."

✳ ✳ ✳

On the morning of the wedding, all Leonato's servants gathered outside the family chapel. Hero looked radiant in her wedding gown, and Claudio and Don Pedro seemed uneasy in their smart

uniforms. Benedick and Beatrice kept glancing at each other and smiling.

The family priest, Friar Francis, raised his hands for silence.

"Friends!" he said.
if anyone knows
of a reason why
this man and
this woman
should not be
married, then—"

"I know a reason!"
Claudio interrupted.
He pointed at Hero.
"She is dishonorable. Last night I saw
her embracing another man."

"You are mistaken!" shouted Leonato.

"No mistake, old friend," said Don
Pedro. "I saw her too. She was on her
balcony kissing Borachio, Don John's
servant. Claudio and I can no longer stay
in this house."

Without a sound, Hero fainted and
collapsed in her father's arms. Beatrice
and Benedick hastened to assist her, while
uproar broke out among the servants.

Don Pedro
and Claudio
marched in step
through the
clamor.
Leonato's eyes
were dazed.
"Can it be true?"
he muttered.

"No, Hero is innocent!" cried Beatrice.

"Of course she is," said Benedick. "This is some trick of Don John's to spite the prince's friend."

Friar Francis crouched down and spoke quietly to Leonato. "Sir, take my advice. Have your daughter carried to her room and announce that she is dead. Claudio will pity her, and pity will rouse loving memories in him.

After a few weeks, when she is restored to him—"

"Claudio doesn't deserve her!" snarled Beatrice. "He should be punished!"

Overcome with emotion, she scampered into the chapel with Benedick close behind.

Beatrice stood before the altar, tears coursing down her face.

"If I were a man, I would make Claudio suffer for what he has done!" she declared.

"I love you more than all the world, Beatrice. I can't bear seeing you so upset," said Benedick. "I would do anything to comfort you."

Beatrice glared at him through her tears.

"Then go to Claudio, tell him that Hero is dead, and challenge him to a duel!" she said fiercely.

* * *

Don Pedro and Claudio were
collecting their horses
from the stables when
Benedick found them.
He ignored their
greetings, seized
Claudio by the
throat, and slammed
him against the
stable door.

"Hero is dead!" he hissed. "Your accusations have cost an innocent lady's life. Name a time and place, and I'll fight you with whatever weapons you choose."

He released Claudio, who stared in bewilderment at Don Pedro.

"Hero—dead?" he whispered.

Cursing voices made the three men turn their heads.

Borachio, with his hands tied behind his back, was being led up to the governor's house by a local constable.

"What's this, constable?" asked Don Pedro.

"I arrested this villain at an inn, my lord," the constable answered. "He was drunk and bragging about deceiving you and Lord Claudio."

Borachio hung his head. "The woman you saw me with last night was Margaret, Lady Hero's chambermaid, dressed in some of her mistress's old clothes," he admitted. "Don John paid me to do it."

"Where is Don John?" demanded Don Pedro.

"He left at daybreak," Borachio said.
"I don't know where he was bound."

"I'll have him hunted down!" vowed
Don Pedro.

Claudio sank to his knees and covered
his face with his hands.

"Hero was innocent—and I killed her!"
he sobbed.

✳ ✳ ✳

That night, a funeral service was held for Hero. Afterward, Claudio and Leonato spoke.

"How can I gain your forgiveness?" said Claudio.

"Nothing will bring Hero back, but there's something you can do," Leonato said. "A poor relation of mine is anxious for his daughter to marry a nobleman.

She's a lovely girl, very like my dear, dead daughter. Will you take her as your wife?"

Claudio, too close to tears to speak, simply nodded.

Early the next morning, Claudio went once more to the chapel to be married. He was met by Leonato, Don Pedro, Friar Francis, Benedick, and Beatrice, who were arm in arm.

"Where is my bride?" asked Claudio.

Hero emerged from the chapel. "Here," she said.

Don Pedro drew a sharp breath. "Can this be the same Hero who was dead?" he wondered aloud.

"She was only dead for as long as her innocence was in doubt, my lord," said Leonato.

Claudio's eyes glowed with love and wonder.

"Hero?" he gasped.

"Take better care of her this time, Claudio, or I'll have to challenge you again," warned Benedick.

He turned to the friar. "Is there room for another couple in your chapel? I asked Beatrice to marry me last night, and she amazed me by saying yes."

Don Pedro laughed.

"Shall I set you up as an archery target, Benedick?" he teased.

"I'm already a target, my lord," said Benedick, grinning broadly, "and all the arrows that struck me were fired by Cupid!"

I do love nothing in the world so well as you:
is it not strange?

Benedick; IV.i.

Love and Lies in

Much Ado About Nothing

Between 1598 and 1601, Shakespeare wrote an amazing ten plays, including *Julius Caesar* and *Much Ado About Nothing*. There was obviously a great demand for new works by him.

Shakespeare probably took the Hero-Claudio plot from a story by the French writer Belleforest. It was common for Elizabethan playwrights to borrow plots—sometimes from one another!

In *Much Ado About Nothing*, Shakespeare writes about the foolish way that people behave when they fall in love. This subject fascinated him, and he returned to it in play after play.

The play shows us how easily we can be made to believe that a lie is true, and that the truth is a lie.

Claudio's love for Hero is sudden and passionate. Convinced that Hero has been unfaithful to him, he cruelly rejects her in public on their wedding day. When he is told that Hero is dead and that he has been tricked, he is plunged into a despair that does not end until he discovers that Hero is alive and that her love for him is miraculously intact.

The love story of Claudio and Hero is overshadowed by the story of Benedick and Beatrice, the reluctant, sharp-tongued lovers. They have to be tricked into realizing what was true all along—that they fell in love with each other the first moment they met.

Shakespeare mixes bitterness into the comedy: Claudio's fury and the seething resentment of Don John, but the audience is never in doubt that the story will end happily. Like the banter between Benedick and Beatrice, the play is a lively game, full of twists, turns, and tricks.

The Taming of the Shrew

A shakespeare story

For Jo, with love
A. M.

RETOLD BY ANDREW MATTHEWS
ILLUSTRATED BY TONY ROSS

cast List

Baptista

A rich gentleman
of Padua

Petruchio

A gentleman
from Verona

Lucentio

A young gentleman
from Pisa

Tranio

Lucentio's servant
and friend

Katherina
The shrew, Baptista's
daughter

Bianca
Katherina's young sister

Hortensio
A suitor to Bianca

Gremio
A suitor to Bianca

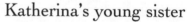

The Scene
Padua in the sixteenth century

Her name is Katherina Minola
Renown'd in Padua for her scolding tongue.

Hortensio; I.ii.

The Taming of the Shrew

Baptista Minola was rich and respectable, but his two daughters were the talk of Padua. The younger, Bianca, was pretty, polite, and modest. Her elder sister,

Katherina, was equally pretty, but her character was completely different. Gossips called her the shrew, a nickname given to any woman with a quick temper and a sharp tongue. As a result, no suitor had asked Baptista's permission to marry Katherina. Bianca, on the other hand, had two suitors: the elderly but wealthy Gremio, and young Hortensio. Katherina was jealous of Bianca, and her jealousy made her more bad-tempered than ever.

One afternoon, two young men who were sightseeing in Padua happened to pass Baptista's house. One was dressed in colorful clothes. His name was Lucentio, the only son of the prosperous Pisan merchant Vincentio.

Lucentio had arrived in Padua that morning and planned to study at the university. The other young man was plainly dressed. He was Tranio, Lucentio's servant and close friend.

Both men were surprised when a door flew open and Baptista burst into the street followed by Gremio, Hortensio, Katherina, and Bianca.

Baptista looked flustered. "You can't make me change my mind!" he said to Gremio and Hortensio. "Bianca won't

marry until Katherina has a husband.
I don't suppose either of you would consider
marrying her?"

"She's too fiery for me!" spluttered
Gremio. "Do you fancy taking her on,
Hortensio?"

"I would rather wrestle with a devil!"
Hortensio replied.

Katherina placed her hands on her hips and glared at her father. "Are you going to let them insult me?" she shrieked.

"I hope you're satisfied, Katherina!" wailed Bianca. "Father is going to shut me away. I'll probably never marry, and it's all your fault!"

This outburst was too much for Baptista. "Enough!" he thundered. "Katherina, Bianca, go inside!"

Bianca burst into tears and fled indoors. Katherina sniffed defiantly and followed her.

"You see the problem, gentlemen?" said Baptista. "If Bianca marries before her sister, Katherina will make my life a misery."

"Are you really going to shut Bianca away, Baptista?" inquired Hortensio.

"I am," said Baptista. "I must hire a schoolmaster and a music teacher to educate her. If either of you hear of someone suitable, please let me know."

Baptista returned to his house, shaking his head and muttering to himself.

Hortensio and Gremio exchanged cold glances. Then Hortensio sighed. "We have been rivals for Bianca's love," he said, "but perhaps we should join forces and find a husband for Katherina. Once she is married off, Bianca will be free to choose between us."

"That's a good idea!" agreed Gremio. "But what kind of fool would want to marry a shrew?"

The two suitors walked off together, deep in thought.

Tranio laughed aloud at the scene he had just witnessed. "I had no idea that Padua was so lively!" he giggled. "Did you notice the expression on the older sister's face?"

Lucentio appeared dazed. "I could only see Bianca!" he gushed. "Her sweet beauty! Her rosy lips! I must woo her!"

"How?" asked Tranio. "You heard her father. He won't let any suitors near Bianca until her sister is married."

"I've got it, Tranio!" cried Lucentio. "We're strangers here. Let's change clothes and places. You can pretend to be me, and ask permission to be Bianca's suitor.  Agree to anything, but make sure Baptista doesn't promise her to anyone else. I'll pretend to be a scholar, take the job as Bianca's teacher, and we'll get to know each other."

"And what then?" said Tranio.

Lucentio grinned. "And then love will find a way!" he said.

✳ ✳ ✳

Hortensio returned home and found an old friend waiting at his front door.

"Petruchio!" exclaimed Hortensio. "What brings you here from Verona?"

"I'm looking for a wealthy wife," Petruchio revealed. "I don't care what she is like, as long as she is rich."

Hortensio wasted no time. He told Petruchio about Katherina and Bianca.

"Hmm!" said Petruchio, with a gleam of interest in his eyes. "I know Baptista well—he is a friend of my father—but I've never met his daughters. What is Katherina like?"

Hortensio pulled a face. "I won't lie to you. She is the worst shrew in Padua," he confessed.

"It will take more than harsh words to put me off!" Petruchio said. "I must see her at once!"

"Can I beg a favor of you?" pleaded Hortensio. "If I put on shabby clothes, will you recommend me as a music master to teach Baptista's daughters? Then I can woo Bianca in secret, while you woo Katherina."

Petruchio was about to agree when Gremio appeared with Lucentio, who was wearing Tranio's clothes and carrying a pile of books.

"I have found a scholar to tutor Bianca," announced Gremio.

"More importantly, my friend Petruchio here is willing to woo Katherina and marry her, if her father gives her a large enough dowry," Hortensio said.

"Are you certain you want to woo
Katherina?" Gremio asked Petruchio.
"She's a wildcat!"

Petruchio thumped his chest. "I've faced
roaring lions, raging seas, and booming
cannon!" he bragged. "I'm not afraid of
Katherina the shrew!"

"Excuse me?" said a voice.

"Does anyone know where Bianca Minola lives?"

Everyone turned and saw Tranio dressed in Lucentio's finery.

Lucentio winked slyly at his friend. "Who are you, and what is your business with Bianca?" demanded Hortensio.

94

"I am Lucentio, and I wish to woo her," Tranio lied smoothly.

Gremio turned red with rage. "Bianca is my chosen love!" he cried.

"Mine too!" added Hortensio.

"Gentlemen!" Petruchio said grandly. "You seem to forget that Bianca won't marry anyone, unless I marry Katherina. Your future happiness is in my hands!"

* * *

95

Not long afterward, Baptista received Gremio, Petruchio, Tranio—who was passing himself off as Lucentio—and the two so-called scholars. After introductions had been made, Baptista sent the tutors away to begin teaching his daughters.

Then
Petruchio
spoke boldly.
"You know
my father,
Baptista, so you
know the kind of
fellow I am. If I marry your daughter
Katherina, what will her dowry be?"

"Twenty thousand crowns and half
my lands when I die," Baptista replied.

"Excellent!" said Petruchio. "The
matter is settled."

Baptista smiled ruefully. "Getting Katherina to agree to the marriage might be more difficult than you think," he warned.

"I'll be more than a match for her!" Petruchio assured him. "I am the breeze that will cool her hot temper."

"Can I discuss Bianca's future with you now, Baptista?" ventured Gremio.

"And I!" broke in Tranio. "I am a newcomer to Padua, but I have already heard of Bianca's grace and beauty. I ask your permission to woo her once Katherina is married." Before Baptista could answer, Hortensio staggered in, with his head sticking out of a broken lute.

"What happened to you?" gasped
Baptista.

"Katherina!" Hortensio groaned.
"When I told her she played badly, she
called me a rascal and smashed this
lute over my head." He wandered off
unsteadily.

"She's a lively one!" chuckled Petruchio.
"I'm longing to meet her!"

"I'll send her to you," said Baptista. "These two gentlemen and I have things to talk over." He led Gremio and Tranio into his study.

Once he was alone, Petruchio paced up and down. "I must confuse her with my wooing," he told himself. "Whatever she says, I'll say the opposite, until she's so mixed up that she won't even notice I've married her!"

Katherina appeared, and for a moment Petruchio was struck dumb by her beauty, but he quickly recovered. "Good day, Kate," he said.

Katherina scowled. "No one calls me Kate!" she snapped.

"I'm going to," insisted Petruchio. "You are the prettiest Kate in the world. I shall marry you and make you *my* Kate."

"Are you a madman who has wandered in off the street?" Katherina fumed.

"No, I'm a gentleman of Verona," declared Petruchio.

"We'll soon see if you're a gentleman!" snarled Katherina, and she slapped Petruchio's face.

Petruchio grabbed her by the wrists and spoke softly to her while she struggled to escape. "I was told you had a bad temper, but you're as sweet as springtime flowers!" he cooed.

Katherina broke free. "You are mad!" she panted.

Baptista stepped out of his study. "How are you two lovebirds?" he asked.

"Do you really want me to marry this lunatic?" screeched Katherina. "What sort of father are you?"

"People are wrong to call your daughter a shrew, Baptista," Petruchio said. "They don't know the real Kate the way I do. We've agreed to be married next Sunday."

"We haven't agreed to anything!" yelped Katherina.

"I must go to Venice for my wedding outfit," Petruchio said. "Until Sunday, Kate." He blew her a kiss and left. Katherina stormed off in the opposite direction.

Baptista returned to his study, where Gremio and Tranio were waiting.

"Bianca's happiness and comfort concern me most," he said to them. "For that reason, if you can prove your father is as wealthy as you claim, Lucentio, Bianca will be your wife."

Tranio bowed. "Thank you, sir," he said.

* * *

On the following Sunday, Petruchio
continued with his scheme to cure
Katherina of her shrewishness
by behaving more
outrageously than
he ever had.
He arrived late at
the church, riding
a scrawny old
horse, and wearing
a hat with a
ridiculously long
feather attached.
His jerkin was
patched, his breeches
were threadbare.
One boot was black,
the other brown, and his
sword was bent and rusty.

During the ceremony, Petruchio bawled out his vows. The priest was so startled that he dropped his book, and when he stooped to pick it up, Petruchio boxed his ears before insisting

on a goblet

of wine, which he spilled over the priest's cassock. Finally, he kissed his new wife with a smacking sound that echoed through the church.

The moment the ceremony was over, Petruchio insisted that he and Katherina should journey to his house in Verona. By the time they got there, Katherina was tired and hungry, but when Petruchio's servants brought food, he said that she could not eat it because it was burned.

When they went
to bed, he
rearranged
all the sheets
and pillows
and was
continually
getting up
to open and
close the
windows,
first saying
that it was
too cold for
Katherina, and
then that it was
too stuffy. In the
end, Katherina was
too weary to complain.

* * *

The next morning, in the garden of Baptista's house, Tranio and Hortensio hid behind a shrub and spied on Lucentio and Bianca, who were seated side by side on a bench.

"Look at how they're holding hands!" whispered Hortensio. "See the way they're gazing into each other's eyes? They're madly in love. Fancy Bianca falling for a penniless scholar!"

"She hasn't," Tranio confessed. "He is Lucentio. I'm his servant, Tranio. We swapped places so that he could woo Bianca."

"And he has won her!" sighed Hortensio. "Oh well! Actually, I've been pretending too. I'm not a music master, but Hortensio, a gentleman of Padua.

Since Bianca has given her heart to another, I'll be off. I know a pretty young widow who would marry me in the twinkle of an eye if I asked her."

Hortensio was proved right, and within a few days he married the widow, and Bianca married Lucentio—the real Lucentio.

* * *

A week later, Petruchio and Katherina visited Padua to attend the party that Baptista threw to celebrate his daughters' marriages.

Though Katherina seemed less stubborn than she had been, Petruchio decided to annoy her to test how well she could keep her temper. When they were almost at Baptista's house, he waved at the sky. "How brightly the moon shines!" he cried.

"The moon?" said Katherina, frowning. "That's the sun!"

"Well, I say it's the moon!" Petruchio declared.

"And I know it's the sun!" retorted Katherina.

"So you still insist on contradicting me, eh?" Petruchio said. "Then let's go back to Verona. We can't stay at your father's house if we're going to bicker all the time."

Katherina hung her head. She was weary, hungry, thirsty, and had been looking forward to being reunited with her family. "All right, Petruchio!" she said meekly. "If you say it's the moon, then so it is."

"Ha, but I say it's the sun!" announced
Petruchio.

"It can be a candle, if you like!" groaned
Katherina. "I don't want to argue
anymore."

Petruchio beamed. "You have no idea
how sweet those words sound!" he said.

* * *

As well as Bianca, Lucentio, Petruchio, and Katherina, Hortensio and his bride were among the guests at the party. Toward the end of the evening, the three new husbands sat drinking together. Wine loosened their tongues and their wits, and they had a disagreement over whose wife was the most obedient.

"Let's settle the matter by each sending a servant to ask our wives to meet us here. The first wife to turn up will be the most obedient." said Petruchio.

"Care to bet twenty crowns on the outcome?" asked Lucentio.

"My Katherina is worth more than a bet of twenty crowns!" Petruchio protested.

"A hundred, then?" suggested Lucentio.

"Done!" agreed Petruchio. "You go first."

Lucentio beckoned to a servant. "Tell your mistress I want to see her right away," he said.

The servant promptly left the room and soon returned. "My mistress says she is too busy to come to you now, sir," he told Lucentio.

Petruchio and Hortensio sniggered at Lucentio's blush.

"Go and ask my wife to come to me!" Hortensio instructed the servant. Once again the servant left, and once again he returned alone.

"Your wife says she is in no mood for jokes, sir," he informed Hortensio. "If you wish to see her, you must go to her."

It was Hortensio's turn to blush.

"Tell Mistress Katherina I wish to see her," Petruchio said to the servant.

For the third time, the servant left, and before long Katherina appeared. "You sent for me, husband?" she said.

"Yes," replied Petruchio. "Find Bianca and Hortensio's wife, and fetch them here." Katherina did as she was told, and within a minute, all three wives stood before their husbands.

"Now, Kate," Petruchio said. "Tell these two headstrong women what you have learned about husbands and wives."

"Our husbands keep us warm and safe and work hard to feed and clothe us," began Katherina, "so we should love, honor, and obey them—not scold them.

We are softer and weaker than men,
and it's foolish to squabble with them.
Husbands and wives should take delight in
one another."

Petruchio laughed and held out his hand to Katherina. "No one will ever call you a shrew again!" he promised. "Come here and kiss me, Kate!"

Why, there's a wench! Come on and
kiss me, Kate.

Petruchio; V.ii.

Love and Marriage in The Taming of the Shrew

Though no one is entirely certain, most scholars agree that Shakespeare probably wrote *The Taming of the Shrew* sometime between 1593 and 1596. He seems to have taken some of the plot from *The Supposes* by George Gascoigne (1566) and may also have been inspired by the ballad *A Shrewd and Cursed Wife* (1550).

Views on marriage have obviously changed a great deal from Shakespeare's time, when a good wife was expected to be meek and obedient, and the husband was very much the head of the household. Today, many would be sympathetic toward the feisty Katherina and would feel uncomfortable about the way Petruchio subdues her.

However, the play is a comedy, and it is difficult to take it seriously because Shakespeare exaggerates things until they become ridiculous. Katherina is a fire-breathing dragon of a shrew—sharp-tongued, vicious, and violent. Petruchio is a posturing macho man with preposterous self-confidence, and some of the methods he uses to tame Katherina are downright silly. Lucentio glimpses Bianca in the street and instantly falls madly in love.

Shakespeare blends their stories into a frothy mixture of disguises, misunderstandings, and romance. As in a pantomime, the audience is never in any doubt that the drama will end happily.

Macbeth

A shakespeare story

For the Michaels
A. M.

For Zoë
T. R.

RETOLD BY ANDREW MATTHEWS
ILLUSTRATED BY TONY ROSS

cast List

The Three Witches or Weird Sisters

Macbeth

Thane of Glamis,
General to King Duncan

Lady Macbeth

Wife to Macbeth

Banquo

General to King Duncan

King Duncan

King of Scotland

Malcolm and Donalbain

The king's sons

Macduff

Thane of Fife

A servant of Glamis castle

Two Murderers

The scene

Scotland in the eleventh century

When shall we three meet again?
In thunder, lightning, or in rain?
When the hurly-burly's done,
When the battle's lost and won.

First and Second Witches; I.i.

Macbeth

All day, the three witches waited on the edge of the battlefield. Hidden by mist and magic, they watched the Scottish army win a victory over the invading forces of Norway, and after the fight was done, they lingered on, gloating over the moans of the dying.

As thunder rolled overhead and rain lashed down, one of the witches raised her long, hooked nose to the wind and sniffed like a dog taking in a scent. "He will be here soon," she said.

The second witch stroked the tuft of silvery hair that sprouted from her chin and grinned, showing her gums. "I hear the sound of hooves, sisters," she said.

The third witch held up a piece of rock crystal in front of her milky, blind eyes. Inside the crystal, something seemed to move. "I see him!" she screeched. "He comes! Let the spell begin."

Two Scottish generals rode slowly away from the battlefield, their heads lowered against the driving rain.

One was Macbeth, the Thane of Glamis, the bravest soldier in King Duncan's army. He was tall, broad-shouldered, and had a warrior's face, broken-nosed and scarred from old fights.

His companion and friend Banquo was younger and slimmer, with a mouth that was quick to smile, although he wasn't smiling now.

Macbeth's dark eyes were distant as he recalled the details of the day's slaughter. "A hard fight to protect an old, feeble king," he thought. "If I ruled Scotland . . ." His mind drifted off into a familiar daydream: he saw himself seated on the throne, with the golden crown of Scotland circling his brow . . .

Suddenly his horse reared and whinnied, its eyes rolling in terror. Macbeth struggled to control the horse, and at that moment a bolt of lightning turned the air violet. In the eerie light he saw three weird hags barring the way, their wild hair and ragged robes streaming like tattered flags in the wind.

Macbeth's hand flew to his sword, but Banquo hissed out an urgent warning. "No, my friend! I do not think  swords can harm creatures like these."

A small, cold fear entered Macbeth's heart, and he snarled to conceal it. "What do you want?" he demanded of the witches. "Stand aside!"

 Moving as one, the witches raised their left arms and pointed crooked fingers at Macbeth. They spoke, and their voices grated like iron on stone.

"All hail, Macbeth, Thane of Glamis!"
"All hail, Macbeth, Thane of Cawdor!"
"All hail, Macbeth, who shall be king!"
Macbeth gave a startled gasp—how had these withered crones come to read his secret thoughts?

The witches turned their fingers to Banquo. "All hail, Banquo!" they chanted. "Your children shall be kings!"

And they vanished like a mist of breath on a mirror.

"Were they ghosts?" Banquo whispered in amazement.

"They were madwomen!" snorted Macbeth. "How can I be Thane of Cawdor? He is alive and well and one of King Duncan's most trusted friends."

"And how could my children be kings if you take the throne?" Banquo asked.

The sound of hoofbeats made both men turn their heads. Out of the rain appeared a royal herald. He pulled his horse to a halt and lifted a hand in salute. "I bring great news!" he announced. "The Thane of Cawdor has confessed to treason and has been executed. The king has given his title and lands to you, noble Macbeth. He has proclaimed you as his heir, after his sons Malcolm and Donalbain. All hail, Macbeth, Thane of Glamis *and* Cawdor!"

Macbeth's face turned deathly pale. "So the witches told the truth?" he thought. "Only Duncan and his sons stand between me and the crown! My wife must know of this—I will write to her tonight."

Macbeth was so deep in thought that he didn't notice the troubled look that Banquo gave him. The witches had left a scent of evil in the air, and Banquo seemed to smell it clinging to his friend.

* * *

Lady Macbeth stood at the window of her bedchamber, gazing out at the clouds gathering above the turrets of Glamis Castle. In her left hand she held the letter from her husband, and its words echoed through her mind. "Glamis, Cawdor, king, you could have them all!" she whispered. "But I know you too well, my lord. You want greatness, but you shrink from what you must do to get it. If only . . ."

There was a knock at the door. Lady Macbeth started and turned, her long black hair whispering against the green silk of her gown. "Come!" she called.

A servant entered. "A message from Lord Macbeth, my lady," he said. "He bids you prepare a royal banquet, for the king will stay at Glamis tomorrow night."

"What?" Lady Macbeth gasped in amazement. "Are you mad?" She quickly recovered herself. "Go and tell the other servants to make ready for the king!" she commanded.

When she was alone again, Lady Macbeth opened the window, and a blast of cold air caught her hair and swirled it about her face. "Fate leads Duncan to Glamis!" she murmured. "Come to me, powers of darkness! Fill me with cruelty, so I may teach my husband how to be ruthless!"

A low growl of thunder answered her.

* * *

Macbeth rode ahead of the king's party and arrived at Glamis just after sunrise. When his wife greeted him, he noticed a hard, determined look in her eyes. "The king sleeps here tonight," he said. "Is his room ready?"

"All is ready . . . for Duncan's last night on earth!" said Lady Macbeth.

"What do you mean?" Macbeth asked.

Lady Macbeth
moved closer
and spoke in
a low voice.
"I guessed the
thoughts that
lay behind your
letter," she said.
"Duncan is old and
weak. His sons are not
fit to rule, but you are! Kill the king while
he sleeps and let Malcolm and Donalbain
bear the blame!"

Macbeth was astonished—first the
witches and now his wife had seen his
innermost thoughts. Some strange force
seemed to have taken control of his life,
and he fought against it. "I will never
commit murder and treason!" he declared.

"I will put a
sleeping potion
in a jug of wine
and send it to
the guards at the
king's door," Lady
Macbeth said quickly.

"They will sleep like babies. It will be
easy for you to slip into Duncan's room."
"No! I cannot!" Macbeth groaned.

Lady Macbeth's
face twisted
into a sneer.
"This is your
real chance to
be king," she
said. "Are you
too cowardly
to take it?"

"I am no coward!" snapped Macbeth.

"Then prove it!" Lady Macbeth hissed.

"Kill the old man and take the throne!"

Once more, the strange force moved through Macbeth, flowing into him from his wife until he was unable to resist. "All hail, Macbeth, who shall be king!" he thought, and he could almost feel the crown upon his head.

＊ ＊ ＊

Long after the castle had fallen silent, Macbeth left his room and crept along the corridors. His hands trembled, and the sound of his pulse in his ears was like the beating of a battle drum. "This is the hour of the wolf and the witch," he thought, "when evil spirits roam the night."

And as the words crossed his mind, a
ghostly glow gathered in the darkness,
shaping itself into a dagger that floated
in the air, shining with a sickly green light.
Macbeth almost cried out in terror.

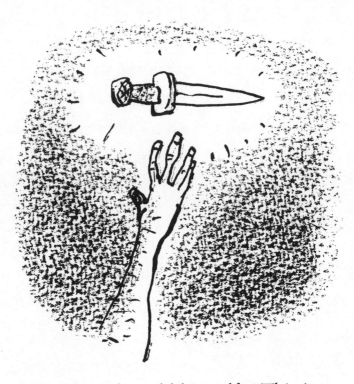

"Be calm!" he told himself. "This is a
trick of the mind!" To prove it, he reached
out his hand to take the dagger, but it
floated away from him and pointed the
way to Duncan's door. Blood began to
ooze from the blade as though the iron
were weeping red tears.

A bell tolled midnight.

"Duncan's funeral bell is ringing!" muttered Macbeth, and he followed the dagger through the gloom.

* * *

Lady Macbeth also heard the bell toll, and it seemed a long time before her husband returned. There was blood on his face and hands, and he carried two daggers.

"You should not have brought the daggers here!" said Lady Macbeth. "Go back and put them into the guards' hands, as we planned!"

Macbeth's eyes were blank. He shook his head. "I will not go back there!" he said hoarsely.

"Then *I will*!" said Lady Macbeth, and she snatched the daggers from Macbeth's hands and left the room.

Macbeth stood where he was, shivering uncontrollably, seeing nothing but Duncan's dead eyes staring. He tried to pray, but his lips and tongue would not form the words.

In a short while, Lady Macbeth came back, holding her red hands up to the candlelight. "I smeared blood over the guards' faces to make them seem guilty," she said. "In the morning, we will have them tortured until they say that Duncan's sons paid them to kill him!"

Her face was so full of triumph and cruelty that Macbeth no longer recognized her. He turned away and caught sight of his reflection in the mirror. It was as if he was looking at someone else—as if he and his wife had become strangers to themselves and each other.

✳ ✳ ✳

Glamis Castle was woken in the gray light of dawn by voices shouting, "Murder! The king is slain!" Shocked guests ran from their rooms and spoke in whispers. Who could have murdered the king?

Rumors flew through the castle like swallows—and suspicion fell on Malcolm and Donalbain, who had the most to gain from their father's death.

Malcolm and Donalbain were convinced that Macbeth was the murderer, but they did not dare accuse him—who would believe that the hero of the battle against the Norwegians would slay his own king?

Though they knew it would be taken as proof of their guilt, Duncan's sons fled for their lives. Donalbain sailed for Ireland,

and Malcolm rode across the border into England to put himself under the protection of the English king.

Now nothing stood between Macbeth and the throne.

He was crowned, but the crown did not
bring him the pleasure he had imagined.
His secret dream had come true, but he
was disturbed by other dreams—dreams
of what the witches had
foretold for Banquo's
descendants.

"Have I lied and
murdered to set
Banquo's spawn on
the throne?" he brooded.
"I must find a way to rid myself
of him and his son."

A dark plan formed in Macbeth's
mind, and he kept it a secret—even from
Lady Macbeth. Without either of them
realizing, the strange force that had
compelled them to kill Duncan was slowly
driving them apart.

∗ ∗ ∗

Macbeth held a coronation feast in
the royal castle at Dunsinane. Many of
the nobles who attended remarked that
Macbeth's old friend Banquo was not
present, but Macbeth laughed when they
mentioned it.

"Lord Banquo and his son must have
been delayed on their way," he said
lightly. Only he knew what had delayed
them, for he had hired two murderers to
ambush them on the road.

At the height of the feast, a servant brought Macbeth a message that two men wished to see him on urgent business. Macbeth hurried to his private chambers and found the murderers waiting there.

"Have you done what I paid you to do?" Macbeth demanded.

"Banquo is dead, my lord," one of the murderers said. "We cut his throat and threw the body into a ditch." Macbeth sighed with relief—perhaps now he would sleep peacefully. But then he sensed something was wrong: neither of the murderers would look at him, and they kept anxiously shuffling their feet.

"And his son?" said Macbeth.

The reply was shattering. "He escaped, my lord. Banquo's son still lives."

As he returned to the banqueting hall, doubts tortured Macbeth like scorpions' stings. "Banquo's son still lives!" he thought. "Lives to take his revenge on me, to claim the throne and father sons who will rule after him. Is there no end to the blood that must be shed before I find peace?"

As he entered the hall, Macbeth put on a false smile to hide his troubled mind; but the smile froze when he saw a hooded figure seated in his chair. "Who dares to sit in my place?" he roared.

The guests fell silent and looked bewildered: the king's chair was empty.

"Why . . . no one, my lord!" said Lady Macbeth with a forced laugh. She could see that something was wrong with her husband, but she could not guess what. "The king is jesting!" she told the nobles.

"This is no jest!" barked Macbeth. He strode angrily toward the figure, then recoiled in horror as it drew back its hood.

For what he saw was Banquo—with
weeds tangled in his hair and mud
streaked across his face, with a deep gash
in his neck that sent a stream of blood
pattering onto the flagstones and haunting,
glassy eyes that stared and stared.

"Get rid of him!" Macbeth screeched.

The nobles sprang to their feet, drawing their daggers, knocking over chairs and wine cups in the confusion.

"Back to your grave!" sobbed Macbeth.

Banquo smiled—there was blood in his mouth, and his teeth shone white through it, then he faded into the shadows and the torchlight.

"My lords, the king is ill," Lady Macbeth said desperately. "Leave us now, and let him rest. In the morning, he will be himself again."

"Myself?" Macbeth moaned softly to himself. "I will not be myself again until Banquo's spirit is laid to rest. Only the witches can set me free!"

✳ ✳ ✳

The witches were seated in a huddle around a fire over which a cauldron bubbled. In the sky above their heads a full moon sailed, casting silver light over the battlefield, still littered with unburied corpses.

The blind witch held up her crystal. Deep inside, a tiny horse and rider galloped wildly through the night. "He comes!" she cackled. "The spell is still strong!"

 And Macbeth came out of the moonlight, his horse's flanks white with lathered sweat. He climbed from the saddle and was about to speak when the hook-nosed witch called out, "The king wishes to know the future!"

"It is not for the fainthearted!" warned the bearded witch.

"I have courage enough!" Macbeth growled.

The blind witch dipped a wooden cup into the cauldron and held it out. "Drink!" she said.

Macbeth took the cup and lifted it to his lips, shuddering as he swallowed.

Fire and ice and the light of the moon burned in his brain.

The blind witch's face melted like the edge of a cloud and became the face of Duncan, his silver hair dark with blood. "Beware Macduff, the Thane of Fife!" Duncan said, and then he changed into Banquo. "No man born of a woman can harm you," Banquo said. "You will rule until Birnam Wood walks to Dunsinane."

"Then I am safe!" cried Macbeth. "No one can stop me!"

And he was alone: the witches, their cauldron, and the fire had vanished.

* * *

It was the start of a fearful time. On his return to Dunsinane, Macbeth ordered that Macduff be arrested. When he heard that Macduff had fled to England to join Malcolm, Macbeth had Macduff's castle burned and his wife and children put to death. From then on, anyone who questioned the king's commands—no matter how harsh or unjust those commands might be—was executed.

The gap between Macbeth and his wife grew wider. The guilty secret of Duncan's murder gnawed at Lady Macbeth's mind like a maggot inside an apple. She fell ill and began to walk in her sleep, dreaming that she and Macbeth were still covered with Duncan's blood. "Out, cursed stain!" she croaked. "Will nothing make me clean?" Doctors could do nothing for her, and she grew weaker every day.

* * *

Then at last hope came to Macbeth's suffering subjects. Malcolm had raised an army in England, and, with Macduff at his side, he marched his troops into Scotland. There the army was greeted by cheering crowds who longed to be freed from the tyrant Macbeth.

First Glamis Castle was captured
and burned, and then Malcolm's forces
marched on to Dunsinane. To the despair
of Macbeth's generals, he did nothing.

Each time they advised him to go to
battle, he laughed and said, "I have
nothing to fear until the day that Birnam
Wood walks to Dunsinane."

* * *

Through the windows of the throne
room, Macbeth could see the distant
campfires of Malcolm's army. He raised a
cup of wine to them. "Fools!" he jeered.
"You cannot overthrow me!"

A sound made him turn. A servant was
standing at the door wringing his hands
and weeping.

"What is it?" Macbeth asked gruffly.

"The queen, my lord," said the servant.
"She is . . . dead."

For a long time, Macbeth was silent, remembering the early years of his marriage, when the world had seemed bright. "Life goes on, day after day, but it means nothing," he said in a cracked whisper. "It ends in despair, and darkness . . . and death."

Macbeth did not sleep that night. He drank cup after cup of wine, but it brought him no comfort. Only the certainty that his enemies would be defeated and that he would remain unharmed gave him any hope.

At dawn, an anxious-faced captain brought the king strange news. "The enemy is approaching, my lord," he said. "To conceal the strength of their numbers, they are hiding behind branches cut from Birnam Wood. It looks as though a forest is on the march."

"My curse upon you, witches!" howled Macbeth. "You deceived me! I have lost everything, but at least I can die like a soldier, with a sword in my hand! Go tell the servants to bring my armor!"

✳ ✳ ✳

It was a short battle. Macbeth's army had no stomach for a fight to protect a king they now hated, and the soldiers began to surrender to Malcolm's men—first in a trickle, then in a flood.

Macbeth fought recklessly, as though he wished to be killed, but he hacked down opponent after opponent, shouting, "You were born of woman!" as he delivered the death blow.

At last, Macbeth found himself alone. He was resting against a cart when he heard someone call his name. It was Macduff, striding through the smoke of battle,  his broadsword at the ready. "I have come to avenge my wife and children!" Macduff said through clenched teeth.

"Stay back!" warned Macbeth. "I cannot be harmed by a man born of woman."

"My mother died before I was born," said Macduff, his eyes blazing with hate. "To save me, the doctor cut me from her body."

Macbeth threw back his head and laughed bitterly. He saw now that all the witches' promises had been lies, and that by believing them, he had betrayed himself. The force that had dominated him was gone, and only his courage remained. "Come then, Macduff!" he cried. "Make an end of me!"

Macduff struck off Macbeth's head with a single sweep of his sword.

* * *

The head was placed on top of a spear that had been driven into the ground outside the gates of Dunsinane. The victorious army cheered, then marched away to see Malcolm crowned king.

As the sun set, three ravens flapped down from the castle walls and fluttered around Macbeth's head. "All hail, Macbeth!" they cawed. "All hail! All hail!"

Out, out, brief candle.
Life's but a walking shadow, a poor player
That struts and frets his hour upon the stage,
And then is heard no more.

Macbeth; V.v.

Evil in Macbeth

Shakespeare wrote *Macbeth* in 1605, four years after James I came to the throne. King James had written a book about witchcraft, and Shakespeare wove three witches into *Macbeth* to flatter the new monarch, who had granted Shakespeare's acting company the title of "The King's Men" in 1603.

Shakespeare's witches do not simply cast wicked spells. Their prophecies and promises play on Macbeth's mind, bringing out a long-kept secret—his ambition to be king.

The evil in the play does not come from the witches, but from Macbeth himself. Urged on by his wife, Macbeth murders the saintly King Duncan, condemns the king's sons as murderers, and is proclaimed king by the Scots noblemen.

Macbeth's dark dream has come true, but his life turns into a nightmare. To keep the throne, he has his best friend murdered and puts to death anyone who dares oppose him. The brave general has become a cruel tyrant.

In the end, Macbeth loses everything. His wife goes mad and dies, and when an English army invades Scotland, his noblemen turn against him. The promises the witches made to Macbeth prove to be hollow, and he dies at the hands of Macduff, whose wife and children he had executed.

With its three witches, a ghost, and a phantom dagger, *Macbeth* was the early seventeenth-century equivalent of a modern horror movie. But the real horror lies in the change that comes over Macbeth's character. The potential for evil, Shakespeare seems to suggest, is lurking inside us all, and we must constantly be on guard against it.

Romeo and Juliet

A shakespeare story

To Leila, with love
A. M.

For Mike and Sue
T. R.

RETOLD BY ANDREW MATTHEWS

ILLUSTRATED BY TONY ROSS

cast List

juliet

Daughter of Lord Capulet

Romeo

Son of Lord Montague

Mercutio

Friend to Romeo

Benvolio

Friend and cousin to Rom[

Tybalt

Cousin to Juliet

Nurse to Juliet

Friar Lawrence

Lord Capulet

The Prince of Verona

A Monk

Messenger to
Friar Lawrence

The Scene

Verona in the fifteenth century

But soft, what light through yonder
window breaks?
It is the east, and Juliet is the sun.

Romeo; II.i.

Romeo and Juliet

On a warm summer's evening, the Capulet house was the brightest place in Verona. The walls of the ballroom were hung with silk tapestries, and candlelight from a dozen crystal chandeliers threw rainbows onto the heads of the masked dancers as they twirled through the music and laughter that filled the air.

On one side of the room, near a table laden with food and drink, stood a young girl, Juliet, the daughter of Lord and Lady Capulet. She had removed her mask and loosened her black hair so that it hung about her shoulders. Her face, flushed from the heat of the dance, was radiant,

and her beauty was obvious to all who looked at her. She seemed unaware that someone was watching her.

A few steps away, a young man stood gazing at her. He had never seen such loveliness before in his whole life.

"Surely I must be mistaken!" he thought. "Surely, if I look a second time, I will find that her eyes are too close together, her nose too long, or her mouth too wide!"

Moving slowly toward her, as one in a trance, the young man lifted his mask so that he could see Juliet more clearly—and the more he gazed at her, the more perfect her face seemed.

Almost without thinking, Romeo
pushed his way toward Juliet until he
found himself standing at her side. Gently
he took her hand.

Juliet turned her head, her soft brown
eyes wide with surprise.

✳ ✳ ✳

On the other side of the room, Tybalt, Lord Capulet's fiery young nephew, recognized the young man who was holding Juliet's hand and strode angrily toward the door. But just as he was about to leave, his uncle caught him by the sleeve.

"Where are you going?" asked Lord Capulet.

"To fetch my rapier," Tybalt replied. "Lord Montague's son, Romeo, has dared to enter the house!"

"Leave him!" said Lord Capulet.

There was a terrible feud between the Capulets and the Montagues, and the Prince of Verona had forbidden any more fighting between the two families on pain of death.

Tybalt's face was ashen with rage. "But tomorrow, Romeo will boast to his friends about how he danced at the Capulets' ball and escaped without being noticed! He will make us look like fools!"

Lord Capulet put his hands on Tybalt's shoulders, forcing him to stop and listen.

"I hate the Montagues as deeply as you do, Tybalt," he said. "Our two families have been at war with each other for as long as anyone can remember—but the prince's word is law in this city, and there is to be no more fighting, you understand? Now, if you cannot keep your temper like a man, go to your room and sulk like a boy!"

Tybalt broke free from his uncle's grasp and glared across the room at Romeo. "You will pay for this one day, Montague!" he vowed softly. "I will make you pay!"

* * *

Juliet glanced at the young man beside her, at his glossy brown hair and startlingly gray eyes that were filled with shyness and wonder. His mouth was curved in a half smile, and though it made her blush to look, Juliet found that she could not take her eyes from his face, or her hand from his.

"My lady," Romeo said, "if my hand has offended yours by holding it, please forgive me."

"My hand is not offended, sir," said Juliet, smiling at him, "and nor am I."

Some power that neither of them understood had drawn them together like a moth to a flame. They kissed and the ballroom, the musicians, and the dancers seemed to disappear, leaving them feeling as though they were the only two people in the world.

When their lips parted, Romeo looked at Juliet and thought, "All those other times when I thought I was in love, I was like a child playing a game. This time I am truly in love—I wonder, could she possibly feel the same?"

Before he could ask, an elderly woman bustled up to them. "My lady," she said to Juliet, "your mother is asking for you."

Juliet frowned, shrugged helplessly at Romeo, and then turned and walked away.

Romeo caught the old woman by the arm. "Do you know that lady?" he demanded.

"Why, sir, she is Juliet, Lord Capulet's daughter," said the woman. "I've been her nurse since she was a baby. And I know who you are, too, young man. Take my advice and leave this house, before there's trouble!"

✳ ✳ ✳

That night, Juliet couldn't get to sleep.
She could only think of Romeo. It was
warm and the moonlight was shining
on the trees in the orchard below. Juliet
stepped out onto her balcony, but she was
so troubled by what her nurse had told
her, that she hardly noticed how lovely the
orchard looked.

"How can I be in love with someone I ought to hate?" she sighed. "Oh, Romeo, why did you have to be a Montague? If you had been born with any other name, I could tell you how much I love you!"

Romeo stepped out of the shadows of the trees into the moonlight. "Call me your love," he said. "It is the only name I want!"

215

Juliet looked down from her balcony and gasped. "How did you get here? If anyone catches you, they will kill you!"

"I climbed the orchard wall," said Romeo. "I had to see you again! I loved you the moment I first saw you, and I want to know if you feel the same."

Juliet's face brightened with joy, then darkened into doubt. "How can I be sure of your love?" she said. "How can I be sure that you will not forget me as soon as tonight is over?" Romeo looked up into Juliet's eyes and saw the way the moonlight shone in them. He knew he would never love anyone else.

"Meet me at Friar Lawrence's chapel at noon tomorrow, and we shall be married!" Romeo declared.

"Married?" laughed Juliet. "But we have only just met! And what will our parents say?"

"Do we need to meet more than once to know that our love is strong and real?" said Romeo. "Must we live apart because of our families' hatred?"

A part of Juliet knew that for them to marry would be mad and impossible, but another part of her knew that if she sent Romeo away now, she might never see him again, and she wasn't sure she could bear that. "Yes!" she said. "Yes, I believe what we feel for each other is true! And yes, I'll meet you tomorrow at the chapel at noon!"

So, the next day, Romeo and Juliet were married.

* * *

The bell in the clock tower of the cathedral tolled twice. The main square of Verona sweltered in the hot sunshine, and the air shimmered. Two young men were lounging beside a fountain, and the taller of

the two, Romeo's closest friend, Mercutio, dipped a handkerchief into the water and mopped his face. "Where is he?" he demanded irritably. "He should have been here an hour ago!"

His companion, Romeo's cousin, Benvolio, smiled at Mercutio's impatience. "Some important business must have detained him," he said.

"A pair of pretty eyes, more like!" snorted Mercutio. But as he glanced across the square, he saw Romeo hurrying toward them. "At last!" Mercutio said sarcastically. "I was beginning to think that the Queen of the Fairies had carried you off in your sleep!"

"I have great news!" said Romeo. "But you must promise to keep it a secret!"

Mercutio looked curiously at his friend. "Oh?" he said.

"I am in love," said Romeo.

Benvolio laughed; Mercutio groaned and shook his head. "You are always in love!" he cried. "A girl only has to look at you sideways to make you fall for her."

"It's more than that this time," said Romeo. "I am in love with . . ."

"Romeo!" interrupted a harsh voice.

Romeo turned and saw Tybalt with a group of sneering Capulets. Tybalt's right hand was resting on the hilt of his sword. "You were at my family's house last night," he said. "Now you must pay for your insolence. Draw your sword!"

Romeo's eyes flashed with anger, then grew calm. "I will not fight you, Tybalt," he said. "It would be like fighting one of my own family."

"Why, you milksop!" jeered Tybalt.

"You're as cowardly as the rest of the Montagues."

"Romeo!" gasped Mercutio. "Are you going to stand and do nothing while he insults your family?"

"I must," said Romeo. "You don't understand. I have no choice . . ."

"But I do!" snarled Mercutio.

His rapier flashed in the sunlight as he drew it. "If you want a fight, Tybalt, I'm your man!" he cried.

In a movement too fast to follow, Tybalt brought out his sword and the two young men began to fight at a dazzling speed.

"Help me stop them, Benvolio!" pleaded Romeo. He caught Mercutio from behind, pinning his arms to his sides. As he did so, Tybalt lunged forward and drove the point of his rapier through Mercutio's heart, fatally wounding him.

"A plague on both your houses," he whispered with his dying breath.

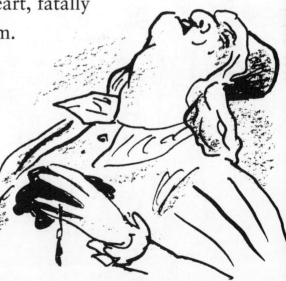

When Romeo realized that his friend was dead, rage surged through him and his hatred of the Capulets brought a bitter taste to his mouth. "Tybalt!" he cried, drawing his rapier. "One of us must join Mercutio in death!"

"Then let our swords decide who it shall be!" Tybalt snarled.

Romeo hacked at Tybalt as though Tybalt were a tree that he wanted to cut down. At first, the watching Capulets laughed at Romeo's clumsiness, but as Tybalt began to fall back toward the center of the square, their laughter died. It was obvious that Tybalt was tiring and finding it difficult to defend himself.

At last, Romeo and Tybalt stood face to face, their swords locked together. Tybalt's left hand fumbled at his belt, and he drew out a dagger. Romeo, seeing the danger, clamped his left hand around Tybalt's wrist, and they stumbled and struggled with each other.

Tybalt flicked
out a foot,
intending to trip
Romeo, but instead
he lost his own
balance and the
two enemies tumbled
to the ground.

Romeo fell on Tybalt's left hand, forcing
the point of the dagger deep into Tybalt's
chest. He felt Tybalt's
dying breath warm
against his cheek.

A voice called
out, "Quick!
The prince's
guards!" and
the Capulets
scattered.

Benvolio helped Romeo to his feet.
"Come now, before it is too late," he said,
but Romeo did not hear him. He stared at
Tybalt's body, and the full realization of
what he had done fell on him like a weight.

"I have killed Juliet's cousin!" he thought. "She cannot love a murderer! She will never forgive me! How could I have let myself be such a fool!"

He was still staring at Tybalt when the prince's guards reached him.

* * *

That night, the Prince of Verona passed judgment on Romeo. "The hatred of the Montagues and Capulets has cost two lives today," he said. "I want no more bloodshed. I will spare Romeo his life, but I banish him to the city of Mantua. He must leave tonight, and if he is ever found in Verona again, he will be put to death!"

* * *

When Friar Lawrence heard the news of Romeo's banishment, he was deeply upset. He had already married Romeo and Juliet in secret, hoping that one day their love would overcome the hatred between the Montagues and the Capulets—but it seemed that the hate had been too strong. After his evening meal, the friar went to his chapel to say a prayer for the young lovers.

As he knelt in front of the altar, Friar Lawrence heard the sound of the chapel door opening and footsteps racing up the aisle. He stood, turned and saw Juliet, who flung herself sobbing at his feet.

"Help me, Friar Lawrence!" she begged. "My father wants me to marry Count Paris, but I'd rather die than forsake Romeo."

"Do not despair, my child," Friar Lawrence urged. "Surely you can reason with your father?"

"I could not bring myself to tell him about Romeo," Juliet sobbed. "I pleaded Tybalt's death had made me too full of grief to think of marriage. But Father would not listen, and the wedding is to take place tomorrow."

Friar Lawrence looked troubled. "There may be a way for you and Romeo to be together, my child, but it is dangerous," he said.

Friar Lawrence took a tiny bottle of blue liquid from the pouch at his belt. "Drink this tonight," he said, "and you will fall into a sleep as deep as death. Your parents will believe that you are dead and will put your body into the Capulet tomb—but in two days you will wake, alive and well."

"And Romeo?" said Juliet.

"I will send him a message explaining everything," said Friar Lawrence. "After you wake, you can go to Mantua in secret."

* * *

And so, on the morning of Juliet's wedding to Paris, the screams of her nurse woke the whole Capulet house.

When the news of Juliet's death reached
Benvolio, he rode straight to Mantua to
Romeo. One of the travelers he passed
on the way was a monk who recognized
him. "Lord Benvolio!" he called out as
Benvolio approached.

"I have a letter for your cousin Romeo
from Friar Lawrence!"

"Out of my way!" Benvolio shouted back. "I have no time to stop!"

The monk watched as Benvolio galloped by on the road to Mantua. At that speed, the monk judged, Benvolio would be in the city before evening.

* * *

When Benvolio told Romeo that Juliet was dead, Romeo's heart broke, and for hours he lay sobbing on his bed, while outside day turned into night. During that time, Benvolio stayed at Romeo's side, but he had no idea how to comfort his grief-stricken friend.

It was almost
midnight before
Romeo grew calm
enough to speak.
He sat up and
wiped away
his tears with
the back of his
hand. "I must go
to her," he said.

"But the prince
has banished you!"
Benvolio reminded him. "If you are seen
on the streets of Verona, it will mean
your death."

"I am not afraid of death," said Romeo.
"Without Juliet, my life means nothing.
Go wake the grooms and tell them to
saddle my horse."

When Benvolio
had left him
alone, Romeo
searched through
the wooden chest
at the foot of his
bed until he found
a green glass bottle that
contained a clear liquid. "I shall drink this
poison, and die at Juliet's side!" he vowed.

Romeo left Mantua at daybreak,
refusing to let Benvolio accompany him.

Once out of the city,
he traveled along
winding country
tracks so that he
could approach
Verona without
being seen.

It was night when he arrived, and with the hood of his cloak drawn up to hide his face, he slipped in unrecognized through the city walls at the main gate.

He went straight to the Capulet tomb, and it was almost as if someone had expected him, for the door was unlocked and the interior was lit by a burning torch.

Romeo looked around, saw Tybalt's body pale as candle wax—then Juliet, laid out on a marble slab, her death shroud as white as a bridal gown. With a cry, Romeo rushed to her side and covered her

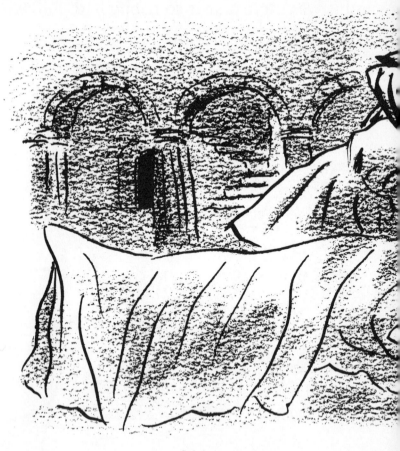

face with kisses and tears. "I cannot live without you," he whispered. "I want your beauty to be the last thing my eyes see. We could not be together in life, my sweet love, but in death, nothing shall part us!"

Romeo drew the cork from the poison bottle and raised it to his lips. He felt the vile liquid sting his throat. Then darkness swallowed him.

For a time, there was no sound except the spluttering of the torch; then Juliet began to breathe. She moaned, opened her eyes, and saw Romeo dead at her side with the empty poison bottle in his hand.

At first she thought she was dreaming, but when she reached out to touch Romeo's face and smelled the bitter scent of the poison, she knew that the nightmare was real and that Friar Lawrence's plan had gone terribly wrong. She cradled Romeo in her arms and rocked him, weeping into his hair.

"If you had only waited a little longer!" Juliet whispered, and she kissed Romeo again and again, desperately hoping that there was enough poison on his lips that she too might die.

Then she saw the torchlight gleam on the dagger at Romeo's belt. She drew the weapon and pressed its point to her heart. "Now, dagger, take me to my love!" she said, and pushed with all her strength.

Friar Lawrence found the lovers a few hours later. They were huddled together like sleeping children.

* * *

When Romeo and Juliet died, the hatred between the Montagues and Capulets died with them. United by grief, the two families agreed that Romeo and Juliet should be buried together. They paid for a statue of the lovers to be set over the grave, and on the base of the statue these words were carved:

There never was a story of more woe
Than this of Juliet and Romeo.

The sun for sorrow will not show his head.
Go hence, to have more talk of these sad things.

The Prince of Verona; V.iii.

Love and Lies in Romeo and Juliet

In *Romeo and Juliet*, Shakespeare weaves together two of the most powerful human emotions, love and hate.

The bitter hatred in *Romeo and Juliet* results from the feud between the Montagues and Capulets, two rich families in the Italian city of Verona. The feud has led to so many gang fights in the streets that the Prince of Verona has ordered the fighting to stop, on pain of death.

The passionate love comes from Romeo and Juliet, who fall in love at first sight at a ball in the Capulets' house. Juliet is a Capulet, Romeo is a Montague, and the moment their lips meet, their fate is sealed. Tybalt, Juliet's cousin, sees them together and swears to take revenge for what he considers an insult to his family.

Shakespeare shows us how strangely alike love and hate are in the way they make people act without thinking. Hate causes the death of both Mercutio, Romeo's best friend, and Tybalt, Juliet's cousin. Love leads Romeo and Juliet into a chain of tragic events. Their happy wedding sets them on the road to a sorry end.

At the end of the play, the young lovers are dead, and the Montagues and Capulets are brought together at last, united by another powerful emotion—grief. The love and the hate have canceled each other out, and all that is left is sadness.

shakespeare stories

RETOLD BY ANDREW MATTHEWS
ILLUSTRATED BY TONY ROSS

As You Like It
Hamlet
A Midsummer Night's Dream
Antony and Cleopatra
The Tempest
Richard III
Macbeth
Twelfth Night
Henry V
Romeo and Juliet
Much Ado About Nothing
Othello
Julius Caesar
King Lear
The Merchant of Venice
The Taming of the Shrew